Arment

D1224851

Eunice Has Everything

Wendy Gless Grant and Sheryl Gless Prutsalis
Illustrated by: Brian Gosselin

Order this book online at www.trafford.com
or email orders@trafford.com

Most Trafford titles are also available at major online book retailers.

© Copyright 2014 Wendy Gless Grant and Sheryl Gless Prutsalis.
All rights reserved. No part of this publication may be reproduced, stored in a retrieval
system, or transmitted, in any form or by any means, electronic, mechanical, photocopying,
recording, or otherwise, without the written prior permission of the author.

Illustrated by: Brian Gosselin

Printed in the United States of America.

ISBN: 978-1-4907-1869-9 (sc)
      978-1-4907-1868-2 (e)

Library of Congress Control Number: 2013923710

Because of the dynamic nature of the Internet, any web addresses or links contained
in this book may have changed since publication and may no longer be valid. The views
expressed in this work are solely those of the author and do not necessarily reflect the
views of the publisher, and the publisher hereby disclaims any responsibility for them.

Any people depicted in stock imagery provided by Thinkstock are models,
and such images are being used for illustrative purposes only.
Certain stock imagery © Thinkstock.

Trafford rev. 01/03/2014

 www.trafford.com
North America & international
toll-free: 1 888 232 4444 (USA & Canada)
fax: 812 355 4082

Eunice was kind, and her heart was quite sweet,
but Eunice could never say no to a treat.
She wanted each toy, and this isn't rare,
but Eunice, you see, received more than her share.
One could say Eunice was overindulged.
Her toy box and closet were stuffed till they bulged.
Her mom loved to please her; her father did too—
if she liked it in pink, then they also bought blue.

Her parents were happy to spoil and adore,
but whatever she had, Eunice still wanted MORE!
For Eunice soon realized that all that it took
was to give a sweet smile and a long, wistful look.
There was no need to beg, no reason to plead.
They'd give her whatever she'd want or she'd need.

Eunice got greedy; she wouldn't deny it.
If it was something she wanted, her parents would buy it.
She had all the latest, the newest, the best.
When she got a new toy, she forgot all the rest.
They piled, they grew, and she loved all her prizes.
She had a fringed skirt in twenty-two sizes.

Inside the house, one hardly could walk
without tripping on Legos, a ball, or a block.
Stacked to the roof there were video games,
tea sets, and books and dolls with no names.
Tinker Toys, Lincoln Logs, dollhouses too.
Crayons and markers and scissors and glue.
There were discarded Barbies in need of some lovin',
a drum set with cymbals, an Easy Bake Oven.
Each room was stuffed from ceiling to floor,
yet somehow they always made room for one more.

And when Eunice decided to go play outside,
there were plenty of options of what she could ride.
A tricycle, a wagon, a unicycle too,
a scooter, a go-cart, but wait—I'm not through!
Roller skates, Rollerblades, ice skates as well,
a skateboard, a bike with a basket and bell!

They never could tell what she would want next—
a laptop, an iPod, a cell phone with text.
Whatever her friends had was what she would fancy.
"I want what Tess has . . . and Carley and Nancy!"
"Life is stupendous!" Eunice shouted with glee.
"For here in my world, the star is just ME!"
She was a tiny bit spoiled, but she didn't quite know it.
She was nice to her friends when she had time to show it.

But Eunice was busy; she was always out buying.
Discovering new things could sometimes be trying.
"I don't have this one!" she would point and exclaim,
as her parents would buy her a new doll or game.
She must have it all, or it just wouldn't do;
if someone else had it, she must own it too!
Her parents grew weary, for it got rather hard.
Her stuff piled up and leaked out to the yard.
"Whatever you want, Eunice dear," they would say,
and whenever she asked, they would say, "Yes, you may."

Now too many yesses for young girls and boys
mean more than too many clothes, games, and toys.
In the world of a child, to hear "No, you cannot"
teaches hoping and wishing for what *isn't* bought.
To hope and to dream are what childhood should be,
but for Eunice, all wishes came true . . . just for free.

Something was missing; she knew it was so—
but Eunice mistook that for somewhere to go.
"Let's go to the circus, the zoo, then the store!
I want a pony, a dolphin, and more!"
Most children return from a trip to the zoo
with a small souvenir, a token or two.
But not Eunice! Oh no—what did *her* parents do?
They brought home a real zebra and a pet kangaroo!

Although she had everything, she was bored as could be.
The void was inside her where she couldn't see.
So she tried to fill it, as any girl would,
with frivolous things, but it did her no good.
"Let's throw a party, I need a new dress!
I need to have more . . . I could never have less!"

Now one time our Eunice was invited to play
at her friend Ruby's house for half of the day.
She was so excited she rushed out the door,
forgetting she wanted to go to the store.
Politely she knocked at the house of her friend,
imagining towers of toys with no end.
"Come in," Ruby said, with a curtsy and smile.
For Ruby, you see, had a very sweet style.

Eunice stepped in, and she looked all around,
but there were no piles of toys or games to be found.
"Hmm..." Eunice thought with a doubt of small measure,
"perhaps in her room is where she keeps all her treasure."
Now Ruby's room, I will tell you, was set up quite nice,
but when Eunice walked in, she had to look twice.
For in this small room, the toys were quite few.
And Eunice thought, "What will we possibly do?"

But Ruby was clever, and Ruby was funny.
"You be the antelope, I'll be the bunny."
This playing was different from what Eunice did.
They laughed and they sang and they danced and
they hid.
The girls got the giggles and whispered some too.
So this is what other girls usually do.
"I love it," thought Eunice, "What a surprise."
"Although there's no stuff, within me the fun lies!"

When she got home, Eunice boxed and she bagged,
she piled, and—oh my!—how those boxes they sagged.
"Not this!" shouted Eunice. "Not that one! Not those!"
She gave away toys and her games and her clothes.
She realized, you see, there was fun to be had,
but fun didn't mean the best item or fad.
Ideas were inside her, but who could have guessed it?
When she played with her friend, she quickly confessed it.

Now don't get me wrong; she kept some of her jewels . . .
and some of her trinkets, but she made up some rules.
She made smart decisions on a practical course.
"Perhaps we don't really have room for a horse.
I don't need eight bikes, and perhaps maybe too
I should not keep the zebra I got from the zoo."
She gave away books; she gave away shirts.
She only kept two of her gorgeous fringed skirts.
Our Eunice got smart and she sent them away
to the needy and hopeful to dress up and play.

Her parents were happy, relieved, and so proud.
To give in excess should not be allowed.
They learned it from Eunice and never forgot.
They could not believe all the things they had bought.
Our Eunice is happy, and when it comes to more stuff—
our girl has now learned when enough is enough.

THE END

CPSIA information can be obtained at www.ICGtesting.com
Printed in the USA
LVOW02s1920050214

372514LV00004B/12/P

9 781490 718699